Big David, Little David

Little David

A Picture Yearling Book

S. E. Hinton

Illustrated by

Alan Daniel

SCHOOL BUS

REGISTER TODAY FOR KINDERGARTEN

...HRIDGE PUBLIC SCHOOL

Published by
Bantam Doubleday Dell Books for Young Readers
a division of
Bantam Doubleday Dell Publishing Group, Inc.
1540 Broadway
New York, New York 10036

ISBN: 0-440-41335-4

Reprinted by arrangement with Doubleday Books for Young Readers

Printed in the United States of America

March 1997

10   9   8   7   6   5   4   3   2   1

To Nick and Big David
with many tricks
on their sleeves
S.E.H.

To Joseph, Kieran,
Ethan, and Dad
A.D.

Nick came home from the first day of kindergarten with a question for his father.

"Dad," Nick said that night as his father was putting him to bed. "Your name is David."

"That's right," Nick's father said. He turned on Nick's night-light. He put Nick's glass of water on the bookcase.

"There's a boy in my class named David," Nick said. "He has black hair, like you. He wears glasses too. He's not you, is he?" Nick asked his question.

"Oh, yes, that's me." Nick's father tucked the blanket around Nick's chin. "See you tomorrow."

Nick's father turned out the big light. Nick wondered until he fell asleep.

The next morning at breakfast, Nick had a question for his mom. But he waited until she finished her coffee. Mom was always nicer when she had finished her coffee.

"Mom," Nick said, "there's a boy in my class
with black hair and glasses
and his name is David.
Is he my dad,
only little?"

"You know your father," Mom said.
"He has many tricks up his sleeve.
Now, go and get your rain boots
and I'll put them on."

"Mom," said Nick, "I think
you're too big for them."

Mom set her coffee down.
"Have I told you
that you're very much
like your father?"

She had.

At school Nick kept staring
at Little David. That couldn't be
his dad. That was a little boy.
But he *did* look like Big David.

Little David noticed Nick staring.
He stuck out his tongue.
Nick called him a bad word.
The teacher wrote both their names
on the bad list. Nick blamed his dad.

That evening he had a test
for Big David.

"Okay," Nick said.
"If you're Little David,
what did we do
in school today?"

"I don't know about you,"
his father answered,
"but I had a hard time with
the Pledge of Allegiance.
The part about the first witch."

"The first witch?" Nick said.
He was having trouble with the
Pledge of Allegiance too.

"You know, 'and to the republic.
First witch it stands.'"

Nick just looked at his father.

"I got in trouble today.
And I'm blaming you."

"Sorry," said his father,
"but when I'm little
I have to act little."

It was just a trick,
Nick decided.
After all, his dad
was a jokester.
Nick wouldn't pay
any attention to
Little David
anymore.

The next day Mom picked
up Nick at school.

"Oh, look," she said, "there's Little David. He's wearing your
green sweat suit. I wish he wouldn't do that. You tear up your
clothes fast enough."

Nick looked at Mom. How did she know that was Little David?
And he *was* wearing a sweat suit just like one Nick had.

"If that's my dad, where's he going?"

"I guess he's going to get big
and go back to work."
"Is he really?" Nick asked.

"What do you think?"

Nick didn't know what to think.

"Sorry I had to borrow your sweat suit," Nick's dad said that evening. "All my little-boy clothes were dirty."

"Don't do it again," said Nick. Then he thought of something.

"If you're Little David," he said, "what did Kelsey do in class today?"

"I hope it wasn't kiss Little David," Mom said. She and Nick's dad traded their newspapers and kept reading.

"You know," said his dad.

"I know *I* know," said Nick. "What was it?"

His dad put down the paper.

"Well, I thought it was pretty funny."

"You thought it was funny that Kelsey threw up? I thought it was gross!"

"Well," said his dad. "You know me."

"Yeah," Nick said. "I know both of you, big and little."

That night after Nick took his shower and got into his pajamas, he asked, "Mom, why does my dad want to be Little David?"

His mom sat on the side of the bed.

"I guess he sees how much fun you're having being a little boy and he wants to have fun too."

"Don't big people have fun?"

"Oh, yes," Mom said. "You know how much fun Dad has when he and his friends watch football."

They did seem to think that was fun, but sometimes they yelled so loud they scared Nick.

"And how much fun he has when he plays on the softball team. It's just hard to play pirates on the playground when you're big. It's hard to even *want* to play pirates on the playground."

Nick tried to imagine Dad and his friends playing pirates on the playground. It was impossible. No wonder he wanted to be little!

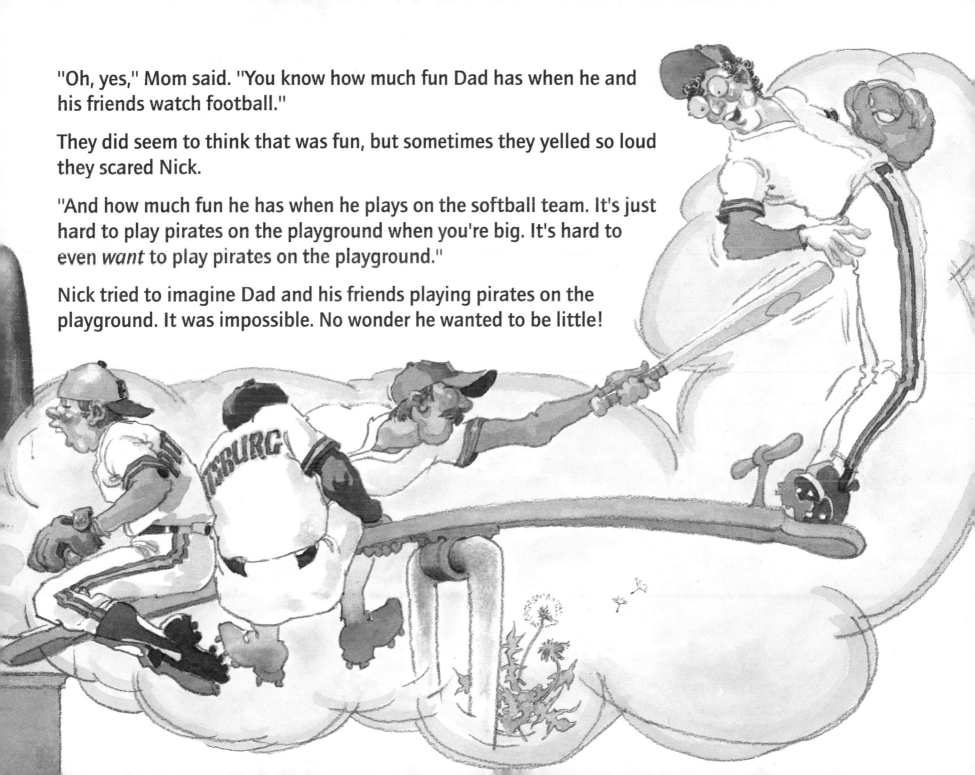

Nick started coming home every day with a new test for his dad. Tests like this:

"If you're Little David," Nick said, "who lost a tooth at lunch?"

"You know," said his dad.

"I know *I* know!" shouted Nick.
"*You* say who," Nick added.
"I'll give you three choose-ments."

"Choices," said his dad.

"Was it Colten?"
asked Nick.

"No."

"Was it Danny?"
asked Nick.
"No."

"Was it Sam?"

"Yes, it was Sam," said his dad.

Nick glared at his dad. How did he know it was always the third choose-ment? "You aren't Little David," he shouted.

"Think about this, Nick," said his dad. "Have you ever seen us together?"

Nick did think about it.
For a long time.

It was Parents' Night at school.

Nick was very excited. He wanted to show his parents his school. He wanted to show them his handprint colored like a turkey. He wanted to show them his classroom and desk and the stars hanging from the ceiling.

"This is my desk," said Nick. He had been so excited to get there, they were early.

"This is my desk," said Big David.

"This is my star," said Nick.

"This is my star," said his dad.

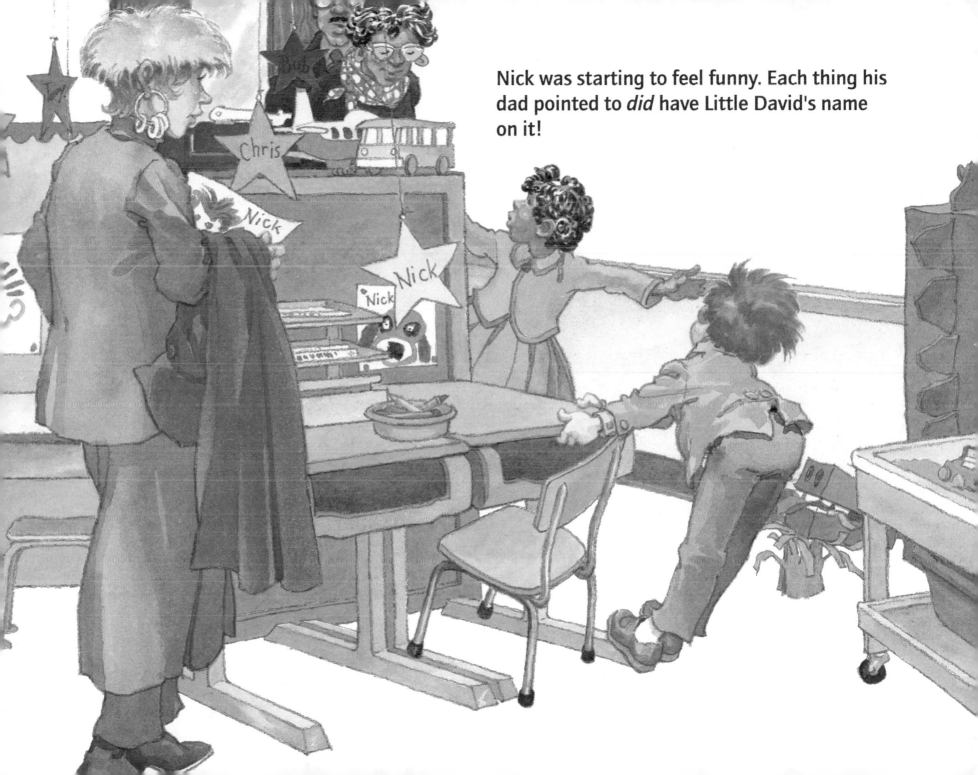

Nick was starting to feel funny. Each thing his dad pointed to *did* have Little David's name on it!

Nick's dad was at the bulletin board.

"Here's my turkey," he said.
"It's not as good as yours."

Nick was feeling very strange.
He didn't want his dad
to be Little David.

Then Little David came in.
He had his parents with him.
His mom had black hair.
His dad wore glasses too.

Nick had seen them together!
They couldn't be the same person!
He was so happy, he laughed.
He had an idea.

He ran to Little David's parents
and hugged them. They were very surprised.

"Grandma!" Nick shouted. "Grandpa!"

Nick's mom said, "Oh, dear,"
and his dad coughed.

Little David said, "That's him!
That's Nick, the boy who
stares at me all the time!"

"I won't stare at you anymore,"
Nick said, and he meant it.
Maybe now they could be friends.

"Good-bye, Grandma. Good-bye, Grandpa,"
said Nick. Little David's parents
were still surprised.

"Excuse us," said Nick's dad.
His face was red.

Outside his parents hurried to the car.
They were very quiet.

"Well, if Little David was my dad,
they would be my grandparents,
wouldn't they?" asked Nick. "Wouldn't they?"

Nick's dad said, "Sometimes
I wonder about you, Nick."

Nick's mom said, "Sometimes
I wonder about the both of you."

Nick just sat back and smiled big.
His dad wasn't the only one
with tricks on his sleeve.

2155-5